For my agent, Susie Cohen —
All my love and thanks
—L B F

For my husband Paul
—T S

Happy Birthday, Mallory!

by Laurie Friedman

illustrations by Tamara Schmitz

Lerner Books • London • New York • Minneapolis

CONTENTS

A WORD FROM MALLORY

Some people might say eight is great, but for me, eight was a really, really, really hard year. Just about everything in my life changed.

First, I had to move to a new town and leave behind my best friend, Mary Ann. Then I had to go to a new school. To top things off, my big brother, Max, got a dog even though we already had a cat . . . my cat, Cheeseburger.

But now I'm turning nine, and I know nine will be great because I'm planning to make nine the best year ever.

To kick things off, I'm planning the best-ever celebration.

It all started tonight when Grandma called.

'I can't believe that in one month, my little Honey Bee will be nine years old. That's so exciting . . . I bet you can hardly wait!'

When Grandma said the part about me being hardly able to wait, I started thinking . . . maybe I shouldn't wait. Maybe I should start celebrating right away.

The more I thought about it, the more I liked the idea. So I made a decision: Starting tomorrow, I'm going to start celebrating.

For my ninth birthday, I'm not going to just celebrate my birth day. I'm going to celebrate my birth *month!*

That's when I realized, I'd better get busy. A birth month celebration takes a lot of planning. But I have a feeling if I plan it all out, it will be the world's best, best, best birth month ever.

Because if you plan it all out, nothing can go wrong.

Right?

A PERFECT PLAN

'Mum, Dad, wake up!' I bounce on my parents' bed until they start to move. 'Do you know what day it is today?'

Mum opens her eyes, but she looks confused. 'Monday?'

'It's Monday,' I say. 'But do you know why this Monday is different than all other Mondays?'

Dad rolls over and looks at the clock on his bedside table. 'Mallory, on all other Mondays, we wake up at seven o'clock. It's 6.15 in the morning! What is so important about this Monday that you needed to wake us up so early?'

I plop down on the bed between Mum and Dad. 'Today is the first day of my birth month celebration!'

I wait for my parents to say, *'Wow, the first day of your birth month celebration. That is so, so, so exciting!'* But that's not what they say.

'What's a birth month celebration?' mumbles Dad.

'It's when you celebrate the *month* you were born, not just the *day*,' I tell him.

Dad rolls his pillow into a ball and puts his head back on it. 'Mallory, a *day* celebration is quite enough.'

'But I want my ninth year to be the best ever, so I'm planning to start it off with the best-ever celebration.' I pull a sheet of paper out of one of my slippers and unfold it. 'I think I've come up with the perfect plan.'

Mum sits up in bed and turns on a light. Dad sits up too. They look at each other, and then they look at me. 'What did you have in mind?' Dad asks me.

I snuggle up between my parents and tell them exactly what I have in mind.

10 Ways I, Mallory McDonald, Plan to Celebrate My 9th Birth Month.

Way 1: By eating ALL the junk food I want.

Way 2: By watching TV for as long as I'd like.

Way 3: By staying home from school on Fridays.

Way 4: By painting my room light purple. (Dad can help.)

Way 5: By not helping around the house. (Max can help.)

Way 6: By getting my ears pierced. (V.I.W.) Very Important Way!

Way 7: By celebrating with a gift-of-the-day.

Way 8: By having a surprise party.

Way 9: By Mary Ann coming to visit on my birthday.

Way 10: By celebrating with a cake-of-the-week.

When I finish reading my list, my parents look at each other like they just came out of a parents' evening at school, and there's something they need to talk to me about.

'Mallory,' says Mum. 'I know you're excited about turning nine. But we need to go through your list and talk about what's reasonable and what's unreasonable.'

'I already went through my list,' I tell Mum. 'I crossed off the unreasonable stuff, like putting a hot fudge fountain in the backgarden.'

Mum reaches for my list. 'I think we better do this together.'

Mum looks at my list. 'Mallory, you can't eat all the junk food you want. You can't watch all the TV you'd like and unless you're really ill, you know you have to go to school *every* day.'

I start to explain that all of these things

are important because they are part of my birth month celebration, but Mum doesn't let me. She looks at my list again and says my name slowly like she's talking to a two-year-old and not an almost nine-year-old.

'MAL-LOR-Y! We just decorated your room. We're not going to repaint it, and your brother does not have to do all your housework for a month. How would you feel if you had to do all of Max's housework for a month?'

I wouldn't want to do that. I don't really want Max to have to do mine, but I don't think Mum understands that a celebration isn't a celebration unless you do something to celebrate it. I point to Way 7 on my list. 'Can I get my ears pierced?'

Mum rubs the sides of her head, like she has a headache that won't go away.

'Mallory, we've talked about this. You can't get your ears pierced until you're twelve.'

'But Mum! Getting my ears pierced is one of the most important ways I want to celebrate my birth month.'

Mum shakes her head. 'No pierced ears!' She hands the list to Dad.

He starts reading. 'A gift of-the-day sounds like a nice idea.' Dad rumples my hair. 'How about a hug and a kiss . . . every day?'

'Not that kind of gift,' I tell Dad.

'Sweet Potato,' says Dad, 'I've never heard of a month-long celebration that includes a gift a day.'

'Let's talk about your party,' says Mum.

'I know you've already planned my skating party,' I say. 'But what I really want is a surprise party.'

'Mallory, you can't plan your own surprise party. If you do, you won't be surprised.'

'I'll act surprised,' I tell Mum. 'Watch.'

I stand up on the bed between Mum and Dad and put my hands on my cheeks. 'I can't believe it!' I suck in air while I'm talking so I don't just look surprised. I sound surprised too. 'All this for *me?*'

I look around the bedroom like I'm looking at friends and presents and decorations that I didn't expect to see. 'I am just so, so, so surprised!'

Dad laughs. 'Mallory, you are very good at acting surprised, but we've already planned your skating party.'

'Turning nine is a big deal,' I explain to Dad. 'I want *everything* to be perfect.'

'*Everything* will be great. We had a skating party for Max when he turned nine,

and it was a lot of fun.'

I look down and pick a fuzz ball off the blanket. 'I want this year to be better than last year, so it's important that it starts with the best-ever celebration. I've told you lots of ways I want to celebrate and you've said *no* to everything.'

Mum looks at the list again. 'Having Mary Ann visit is a nice idea. I'll call her mum and see if they can come down for your birthday weekend.'

'I hope she can come.' I look down and pick another fuzz ball off the blanket. 'I can't imagine my birthday without my best friend.'

'I'll call her mum today,' says Mum.

Dad clears his throat like he's a judge and he's about to say something important to the jury. 'Mallory, celebrations are nice, but whatever you do to celebrate your birthday won't affect the way your year turns out.'

I know you're not supposed to argue with a judge, but I think Dad is wrong.

'Dad, it's like revising for an exam,' I say. 'If you study, you get a good mark. If you plan a good celebration, you have a good year.'

Dad pats me on the head, like he heard what I said but he doesn't agree. 'I think we've had enough birthday talk for one morning. Why don't you go and get dressed?'

I start to go downstairs. Then I stop.

'Wait a minute,' I say. 'What about Way 10? Celebrating each week of my birth month with a cake-of-the-week?'

Mum laughs. 'A cake a week sounds like a sweet idea.'

I can't believe Mum said *yes* to something.

'Can we have a cake on Saturday?'

'I don't see why not,' says Mum.

Now it's my turn to smile. 'Can we have chocolate cake with fudge icing and coloured sprinkles?'

'Sounds like a plan,' says Mum. 'Now go and get ready for school.'

'OK,' I tell Mum, but as I walk down the stairs, there's only one thing I can think about getting ready for and that's my birth month celebration.

I've got a lot to do if it's going to be the best, best, best celebration ever.

MALLORY ON A MISSION

I'm on a mission. A *make-sure-everybody-knows-it's-my-birth-month* mission. There are a lot of people who I want to be part of my celebration. I split my mission into five parts.

MALLORY'S MISSION: PART I
Target: My brother, Max
Location: Our bathroom sink

When I walk into the bathroom, Max is already brushing his teeth. His dog, Champ, is with him.

I squirt toothpaste onto my toothbrush. 'Guess what?' I say to Max. 'I'm celebrating my birth month this year, not just my birth day, and today is the official start of my celebration.'

Max spits into the sink. 'Guess what? I'm skipping school and going fishing.'

Sometimes Max says such stupid things.

'You can't skip school and go fishing.'

'Well, you can't celebrate your birthday for a month.' Max wipes off his mouth with the back of his hand.

'Give me three good reasons why not!'

Max rolls his eyes. 'Because it's silly, because it's stupid, and because Mum and Dad won't let you.'

I finish brushing and stick my toothbrush into my hole in the toothbrush holder.

'Mum already said I can have a cake a week during my birth month. I'm having my first cake on Saturday and since you're my only brother, I want to make sure you'll be there to wish me *Happy Birth Month*.'

I reach down and stroke Champ. 'He's invited too.'

'Did you say you're having a cake a week for your birth month?'

I nod.

'And Mum agreed to that?'

I nod again. 'Max, I'm turning nine. This is a very important celebration.'

Max rolls his eyes again. 'I'm turning eleven and you don't see me celebrating my birthday for a month. The last time I checked, nine was hardly a big deal.'

Max might not think nine is a big deal now, but he will on Saturday when he has a big piece of chocolate cake on his plate.

Part I of my mission is complete. On to Part II.

MALLORY'S MISSION: PART II
> *Target:* *My next-door neighbours, Joey and*
> *Winnie Winston*
> *Location:* *On our way to school*

'Knock, knock,' I say as we walk towards Fern Falls School.

'Who's there?' asks Joey.

'Itzmy,' I say smiling.

'Itzmy?' Winnie repeats the name like it's the title of a boring book she has to read for school and not the first part of a knock-knock joke.

Joey ignores his sister. 'Itzmy who?' he asks.

'It's my birth month celebration starting today,' I tell them. 'I'm having a cake a week. My first one is on Saturday and you're both invited.'

Winnie's lip curls up like a sleeping bag. 'Who ever heard of celebrating a birth month? Count me out. I've got more important things to do, like brush my hair.' Winnie walks ahead of Joey and me.

I look at Joey. 'Can you come on Saturday?'

'I don't know,' he says. 'I'm supposed to go ice skating with Pete on Saturday.'

'C'mon! I'll make sure you get an extra-big piece.'

Joey's been a great friend ever since I moved to Fern Falls. I know he'll be there.

Part II of my mission is complete. Now, it's time for Part III.

MALLORY'S MISSION: PART III
Target: My class mate, Pamela
Location: Fern Falls School, Room 310
As soon as I walk into my classroom, Mrs Daily tells us to open our science books to page ninety-six. 'Today, we're starting our unit on astronauts and space,' she says.

I open up my science book and turn the pages slowly. It's not that I mind learning about astronauts and space, but what I really want to do is invite Pamela to my birth month celebration.

I just don't want to celebrate without her.

Mrs Daily starts reading about rockets. I start a note to Pamela.

Pamela,
I am celebrating my birth month, which starts TODAY!!!!!!
Can you come to a celebration at my house on Saturday?
Hugs, Mallory

I fold my note into a tiny square and pass it to Pamela. When she's read it, she turns it over and writes something on the back, then refolds the piece of paper and passes it back to me.

Mallory,
Happy birth month!
I would love to help you celebrate, but I have a violin lesson on Saturday.
I have to talk to my mum.
Hugs back, Pamela

When I finish reading, I smile at Pamela. '*See you Saturday,*' I mouth to her.

I know Pamela's mum will let her come to my house. Everyone knows a birth month celebration is a lot more important than a violin lesson.

Part III of my mission is complete. On to Part IV.

MALLORY'S MISSION: PART IV

Target: Grandma

Location: On the phone

When I get home from school, I don't even stop for a snack. I go straight to the phone and dial Grandma's number.

When she answers, I tell her right away about the special celebration I have planned. 'Grandma, I decided to celebrate my birth month this year!'

Before Grandma has a chance to say anything, my birth month plans start spilling out of my mouth like chocolate chips falling from an open bag. 'I'm having a cake a week and Mary Ann might come to visit and I'm having a party!' I tell her.

'Slow down,' says Grandma.

But once I get started, it's hard to slow down. 'Even though I really wanted to have a surprise party, I'm having a skating party. I know you live a long way away, but I wanted to know if you can come to my party.'

Grandma sighs into the phone. 'Honey Bee, I do live a long way away, but I'm planning to send you something special for your birthday this year.'

I smile into the phone. 'Can you give me a hint about what you're sending?'

Grandma laughs. 'No hints. But I think you'll like it.'

Knowing Grandma, I'm sure I will. I say goodbye to Grandma, then I head to my room. There's still one very important person that needs to know about my birth month celebration.

MALLORY'S MISSION: PART V
Target: My best, best, best friend, Mary Ann
Location: My desk in my room

Dear Mary Ann,

I have something important to tell you. I'm celebrating my birth month this year!

I know that's not something we've done before, but I decided to do things differently this year.

If you're wondering why, I'll tell you.

Being eight was my worst, worst, worst year ever!!! If I had to rate it, I'd give it a big thumbs-down. (moving and leaving you was the worst part!)

I want to make nine the best year ever, so I'm planning to start it off with the best-ever celebration!

Even though mum said no to lots of ways that I want to celebrate, like getting my ears pierced (she said I have to wait until I'm twelve) and having a surprise party (she already planned a skating party), she said yes to you coming to visit on my birthday!

I hope your mum says you can come!

WRITE TO ME AS SOON AS YOU KNOW IF YOU ARE COMING!

Biggest, hugest hugs and kisses ever, mallory

PS Here's something mum said yes to: a cake-a-week for my birth month! This Saturday I'm having my first cake, chocolate with sprinkles! It will be great except for one thing: NO YOU! BOO-HOO!

I finish my letter and stick it in an envelope. Max, Joey, Winnie, Pamela,

Grandma and Mary Ann all know about my special celebration. Now I feel like my birth month can begin. I put my hands behind my head and my feet on my desk, like I've seen detectives do on TV when they crack a case.

'Cheeseburger,' I say to my cat, 'mission accomplished.'

SADDER DAY

'AH-CHOO!'

That makes sixty-seven times Mum has sneezed since she woke up this morning. I walk into her room with a box of tissues.

'AH-CHOO!'

Sixty-eight.

I hand Mum the box.

Mum looks at me. At least she tries to look at me, but her eyes are all puffy and swollen from coughing and sneezing.

'Mallory, I know you're disappointed. I'm sorry today isn't going like you wanted it to.'

Mum is right. Today *isn't* going like I wanted it to. Today is Saturday, but it should be called '*Sadder Day.*' Today is a whole lot sadder than I thought it would be.

Today is the day I was supposed to be enjoying a cake-of-the-week with my friends and family. Right now, my mouth should be filled with the taste of chocolate cake and fudge icing, but right now, my mouth is empty.

'Don't look so glum,' says Dad. He walks into the room and hands me an envelope with my name on it. 'The postman paid you a visit.'

I take my envelope, walk into the kitchen and sit down at the table.

I didn't get a cake-of-the-week, but at least I get a letter from my best friend.

Dear Mallory,

Happy, happy, happy birth month!!!!!!

Are you having the best birth month ever? I bet you are.

I have some very happy birth month news that I know you will like hearing.

I'M COMING TO VISIT! Did your mum tell you yet? My mum said we can come for your whole birth weekend! (I decided there must be such a thing as a birth weekend since there is such a thing as a birth month.)

I wanted to come for the whole month. Mum said no to that, but she did say I will be there for your skating party! I am so, so, so excited! I don't think it matters that you're not having a surprise party. Skating parties are fun, too!

See you soon, soon, soon!

Hugs and kisses,

Mary Ann

PS How was your cake-of-the-week?
I want to hear about it, down to the very last
sprinkle.

PPS I hope you took
pictures when you blew
out your candles. When
I come and visit, we
can make a birth
month scrapbook.

PPPS Tell your mum that nine is OLD to
get your ears pierced. I got mine pierced
when I was eight. Remember? Maybe you
should try asking your mum in a different way.
I just know she'll say yes!

I reread the letter from Mary Ann. Then
I take a sheet of paper from Mum's desk
and start writing.

Dear Mary Ann,

I have some bad, bad, bad news.

My birth month isn't going like I had planned.

It's a long, sad story, but since you're my best friend, I'll tell it to you anyway.

I didn't get a cake-of-the-week because Mum didn't bake a cake-of-the-week because she has the flu.

Even if she had baked it, no one would have come to eat it, because Joey had other plans and Pamela had a violin lesson and Max and Winnie both said it was silly.

Since I didn't have a cake, I don't have any pictures to put in my birth month scrapbook.

I hope this story did not make you too sad. I am counting the days and minutes and seconds until you get here.

Mallory

PS mum hasn't said yes to getting my ears pierced yet, but I think she will. (See plan below for how I'm going to ask her.)

Operation Earrings

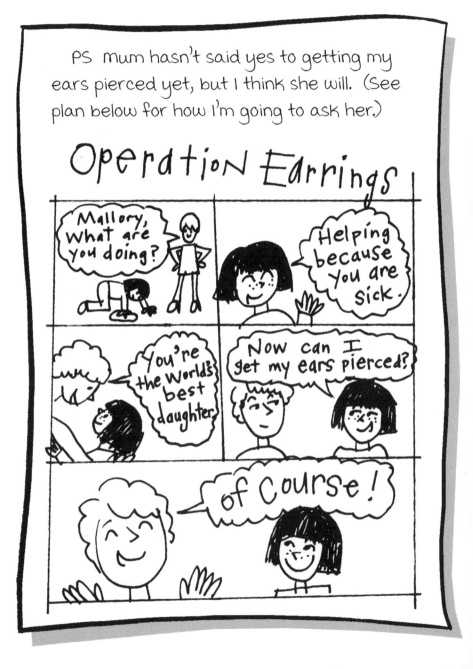

I finish my letter to Mary Ann, fold it, and stick it in the envelope.

The first week of my birth month wasn't so great. I try not to think about what *didn't* happen and instead think about all the good things that are *going* to happen.

I think about the cake-of-the-week I'm going to have next week. I think about the class party I'm going to have the week after that. I think about Mary Ann coming to visit. Then, I think about how much fun it will be to have pierced ears.

I reach up and feel the soft, floppy part of my earlobes.

Tonight . . . I will put Operation Earrings into action.

Tomorrow . . . there will be holes where today there were none.

THE HOLE STORY

'Good morning, class,' says Mrs Daily. 'How was everyone's weekend?'

Room 310 fills up with *goods* and *greats* and *supers* and *terrifics*. There are even a few *amazings*. I keep quiet though. I wouldn't describe the first weekend of my birth month as good or great or super or terrific and definitely not amazing.

'What did everyone do?' asks Mrs Daily.

'I went ice skating,' says Joey.

'Me too,' says Pete.

'I took a violin lesson,' calls out Pamela.

'We went shopping,' says Danielle.

'Shoe shopping,' says Arielle.

Both girls stick their feet in the air to show the class their matching trainers.

Mrs Daily smiles at Danielle and Arielle's feet.

Then she smiles at me. 'Mallory, what did you do this weekend?'

All I can think about is what I *didn't* do. 'Nothing,' I mumble.

'Well, I'm sure you did something,' says Mrs Daily. She picks up a marker pen and writes *What I Did This Weekend* on the board.

'Class, this morning, I'd like you all to write a one-page story about what you did this weekend. Use details about what happened to make the reader feel like they were there with you.'

Everyone takes out paper and pencils, but not me. I don't get out anything to write with because I don't have anything to write about. Mrs Daily comes over to my desk. 'Having trouble getting started?'

I nod.

'Think for a minute,' says Mrs Daily.

'You'll come up with something.'

'I know what Mallory can write about,' says Pamela. 'She's turning nine soon. She can write about what she did this weekend to celebrate her birthday.'

Pamela winks at me like she knows what I did this weekend, but what Pamela doesn't know is that I didn't do anything.

Mrs Daily clears her throat. 'Mallory,

what do you think of that idea?'

I think about my weekend. I didn't get a
cake. I tried to talk to Mum about getting
my ears pierced, but that didn't work
either.

'Mrs Daily, would it be OK if I write about
what I *didn't* do this weekend?'

Mrs Daily says if that's what I remember
about my weekend, then I can certainly

write about it. I take out a sheet of paper and begin.

The Hole Story
By Mallory McDonald
Author's Note: You will need tissues when you read this story. It is very sad!

Once upon a time, there was a little girl who was about to turn nine. All she wanted for her birthday were two little holes, one in each ear. So one weekend, she asked her mother if she could get these two little holes.

Her mother said, 'NO! You may not have two little holes, one in each ear, until you turn twelve.'

So the little girl did what any other little girl who was about to turn nine (and wanted something really, really, really badly) would do.

She begged and pleaded with her mother.

Her mother still said, 'NO!'

So then, the little girl scrubbed the floor. That was how she spent her weekend. SCRUBBING THE FLOOR! She hoped this would get her mother to change her mind.

But guess what? It didn't work. Her

mother still said, 'NO!' (This was mean and cruel of her mother, don't you think?)

So the little girl offered to pay for the holes in her ears with her very own pocket money and eat spinach if her mother would just let her get those two tiny, little holes. But her mother still said, 'NO!'

The little girl was starting to think things were hopeless, but she didn't give up.

She told her mother that the *only* thing she would need to make her birth month (which hadn't been so great so far) extra-special would be those two little holes.

You won't believe what happened next.

You will never EVER guess.

Her mother still said, 'NO!' To top it off, she sent the girl to her room for not listening the first time.

When that happened, a tear ran down the girl's cheek. She had no choice but to wipe it away and move on with her life.

The moral of the story is that mothers should not say no to their children because it makes them very sad.

The End

When I finish my story, I look at my classmate. Pamela is still busy writing. I put my head down on my desk. I knew my birth month wasn't going so well, but I didn't realize how bad it was until now.

I close my eyes and do what I do when I

want something to happen and I'm not sure it's going to. I pretend that I'm at the wish pond on my road and I make a wish.

I wish that the second week of my birth month will be better than the first week.

I try to draw a picture in my brain of the cookie cake with rainbow writing that I want for my second cake-of-the-week. When I know exactly what it looks like, I pretend to throw a wish pebble in the wish pond.

I really hope my wish comes true.

HALF-BIRTHDAYS

Grandma says when you're waiting for something to happen, time goes slowly. She says there's a clock fairy that sits on the hands of the clock to slow them down.

The clock fairy must have been sitting on my clock because this week felt like the slowest week of my life. I never thought today would get here.

I sit up in bed and look at my calendar. 'Cheeseburger,' I say to my cat, 'this Saturday is going to be different from last Saturday.'

Last Saturday, I was sad, sad, sad. Just thinking about the chocolate cake with fudge frosting that I didn't get makes me feel like staying in bed. But this Saturday, I'm happy, happy, happy. I'm celebrating my birth month with a chocolate cake with rainbow writing!

I scoop up Cheeseburger, jump out of bed and skip into the bathroom.

I open up my hair-thingies drawer and pull out my rainbow ribbon. I put my hair in a ponytail and tie the ribbon around it. When I'm finished, I look in the mirror. 'My hair will match the icing on my cookie cake,' I tell Cheeseburger.

I tuck her under my arm and skip down

the hall into the kitchen.

Mum smiles when she sees me.

'Mallory, I'm glad it's you. Would you like to help me bake a cake?'

Someone should give Mum a T-shirt that says '*Mind Reader.*'

'That's exactly what I'd like to do!'

'I was hoping you'd say that,' says Mum. She opens up her cookbook and starts taking ingredients from the larder. Flour, sugar, vanilla, coconut.

I pick up the bag of coconut. I love cookie cake, but I hate coconut. I'm surprised cookie cake has something in it that I hate.

I look at the recipe in Mum's cookbook, and when I do, I get another surprise. 'Mum, this isn't a recipe for cookie cake. This is a recipe for coconut cake.'

Mum takes eggs and butter from the

refrigerator.

'You know I don't like coconut, so why would you bake a coconut cake for my cake-of-the-week?' I say to Mum.

'Mallory, this cake is for Winnie,' says Mum. 'We're invited to the Winstons' tonight to celebrate her half-birthday. Mr Winston asked if I would bake a cake.'

This cake wasn't supposed to be for

Winnie! 'Mum, why are we celebrating Winnie's birthday, which is half a year away, when my birthday is in less than two weeks?'

Mum puts the eggs and butter down on the counter. 'Winnie will be at summer camp on her real birthday, so she wants to celebrate her half-birthday at home.'

'Why don't we make two cakes?' I say to Mum. 'We can celebrate Winnie's half-birthday and my birth month.'

Max walks into the kitchen and grabs a banana. 'Enough with the birth month stuff,' he says. 'It's getting stupid.'

I put my hands on my hips. 'If you think celebrating my birth month is stupid, I bet you think celebrating Winnie's half-birthday is really stupid.'

Max takes a bite of banana. 'That's different.'

I don't see what's different about it. I march over to where Mum is mixing. 'You said I could have a cake-a-week for my birth month, remember?'

Mum stops mixing. 'Mallory, I never said you could have a cake-a-week.'

'You said it was a sweet idea.'

Mum takes a deep breath. She says my name slowly like she has something to tell me and she isn't sure where to start. 'Mal-lor-y, I think we've had a misunderstanding. Having a cake is always a fun thing to do, but I didn't mean you could have one every week.'

'Can I have one tonight?'

'Tonight is Winnie's night. We're going to the Winstons' house for her celebration.' She drops the butter into the mixer. Then she continues talking. 'You have a lot to look forward to. Next Friday is your class party. Then, Mary Ann and her mum are coming to visit us, and, you're having a skating party.'

I start to explain to Mum why she's not being fair, but she gives me a *that's-the-end-of-this-discussion* look. She pours some sugar into the mixer and turns it on.

I go into my room and sit down on my bed with Cheeseburger.

I think about my birth month. It isn't going the way I wanted it to. Just thinking about it gives me a funny feeling . . . and that feeling stays with me all day. I still have it as we walk next door to the Winstons' for Winnie's half-birthday party.

'Welcome,' Mr Winston says to Mum, Dad, Max and me when he answers the door. 'What a beautiful cake,' he says to Mum when he sees what she's holding.

I look at the words *Happy Half-Birthday,*

Winnie on the top of the cake. I can't help wishing they said *Happy Birth Month, Mallory*.

Mr Winston pats me on the head. 'Joey's in his room. Why don't you go and get him and come to the kitchen. Then the party can start.'

I walk down the hall to Joey's room. His

door is open, so I walk in. 'Ready for Winnie's party?'

'Yeah,' Joey says. Then he points to a calendar on his wall. 'I'm ready for your party too. Just one week and two days until we go skating.'

I shrug my shoulders.

'Aren't you excited?'

I don't want Joey to think I'm unexcited to have a party, so I explain. 'The thing is, I really didn't want a skating party. I don't even have my own skates.'

'You can rent skates at the skating rink,' says Joey. He smiles like he has all the answers. 'See, no problem.'

Joey says 'no problem' like my birthday is going to be great. The thing is, I don't feel like it's going to be great. I don't feel like anything is going the way I wanted it to.

When we walk into the kitchen, balloons and streamers are hanging from the ceiling. There's a sign on the wall that says *Happy Half-Birthday, Winnie!* Two big boxes wrapped in yellow tissue paper are sitting on the worktop.

'We have everything Winnie likes tonight. Pizza, spaghetti and Caesar salad,' says Mr Winston.

Joey points to the boxes on the counter. 'Presents too.'

Winnie smiles like she's really happy. Usually, she only smiles if somebody else does something stupid. 'Dad,' she says, 'can I open my presents now?'

Mr Winston laughs. 'How about after dinner?'

Everybody takes plates and piles them high with pizza, spaghetti and salad. I love pizza, spaghetti and salad, but tonight, I

put just a little of each on my plate.

Joey looks at the single strand of spaghetti on my plate. 'Mallory, is that all you want? I thought spaghetti was one of your favourites.'

I look down at my plate. 'I'm not very hungry.'

Joey pretends to feel my forehead. 'You're not getting ill are you?'

Joey is not a doctor. I shake my head *no* and move his hand.

'Pre-birthday jitters?' he asks.

I know Joey is trying to be funny and make me laugh, but I don't. I shake my head *no* again.

Mr Winston looks concerned. 'Mallory, is something wrong?'

I wasn't going to bring this up, but since he asked, I explain. 'It's just that tonight, I was supposed to . . .'

Before I can even say the words *celebrate my birth month*, Dad stops me.

'Everything is fine,' says Dad. He gives me a *stop-talking-and-start-eating* look. Mum looks at me too, like she can't believe what I was about to say.

I stick my fork into a piece of lettuce and chew my Caesar salad in silence. I feel like nobody, not even Mum and Dad, cares about celebrating my birth month.

After dinner, we sing *Happy Half-Birthday* to Winnie. Even Max, who never sings, sings. Winnie blows out her candles, then she opens her presents.

She gets a new jumper from her dad and a matching hat and gloves from Joey.

She pulls her hat on her head to model it. 'I love everything!' says Winnie.

Everyone is smiling.

I try to smile too, but my mouth is

having a hard time cooperating.

'Can we cut the cake now?' asks Winnie.

Mum slices and Joey passes around plates.

I look at Mum. She gives me a slice of coconut cake and a *don't-be-rude* look.

I think about the piece of cookie cake that should be on this plate and even though I hate coconut cake, I do something I never thought I was going to have to do during my birth month . . . I take a bite.

There's only one thing worse than a birth month that isn't going like you wanted it to . . . and that's a mouthful of coconut.

PARTY POOPED

'MUM! DAD! COME QUICK!' I yell from my bedroom.

I hear Mum and Dad running down the hall. They're in my bedroom in less time than it takes to sneeze.

'Mallory, what's the matter?' asks Dad. He's out of breath.

I hold up a purple turtleneck with tassles and a pink jumper covered in hearts. 'Which one do you think I should wear?'

Mum and Dad look at each other, then Dad puts his hands over his heart. 'Phew!' he says. 'I thought something was wrong.'

I put my hands on my hips. 'Something is wrong! I can't decide which outfit to wear for my class party today. I don't want to pick the wrong one!'

Mum smiles. 'I'm glad to see you're so excited.'

I look in the mirror and hold my two

outfits up to my face. Then I smile at Mum.

'Of course I'm excited! I just don't know how I'm going to be able to wait until you and Dad get to my classroom this afternoon with the fairy cakes.'

Dad laughs. 'Visions of pink fairy cakes will be dancing through your head.'

'That's it!' I tell Dad. 'You just gave me a great idea!' I stick the purple turtleneck back into my drawer and pull the pink jumper over my head. Then I pull on the matching pink trousers. 'I'll wear pink, so I match my fairy cakes.'

'Glad I could help,' says Dad. He kisses my forehead. 'I've got to go to work, but I'll see you this afternoon.'

Mum ruffles my hair. 'Hurry,' she says. 'You don't want to be late for school.'

Mum is right. I don't want to miss a minute of what I know will be the best day yet of my birth month.

I go into my bathroom. I tie a big pink bow in my hair and pull a handful of pink stretchy bracelets over my wrist. 'Now I'm perfectly pink!' I tell Cheeseburger. I pick up my cat and walk into the kitchen.

Max is already at the breakfast table with Champ. When I walk in, he looks up and laughs. 'Did you fall into a bucket of pink paint?'

I take a slice of toast out of the toaster and sit down at the breakfast table. 'For your information, I picked pink on purpose.'

Max looks at me like that makes about as much sense as choosing a day-old doughnut. 'Why would anybody pick pink on purpose?'

I think about the vanilla fairy cakes with strawberry icing that Dad is picking up from the cake shop this afternoon. 'My class party is today, and I'm wearing pink so I'll match my fairy cakes,' I tell Max.

Max laughs, and when he does, little bits of toast fly out of his mouth and land on his plate. 'I've heard of eating fairy cakes, but I've never heard of matching them.'

Champ licks Max's plate.

Mum passes Max a napkin. 'Today is a special day for Mallory.'

Mum is right. Today is special, and I don't want anything to go wrong. 'Can we go over the plan again?' I ask.

Mum nods.

'Dad is picking up the fairy cakes from the cake shop this afternoon?'

Mum nods again.

'And you're bringing everything else?'

'I've got it all,' says Mum. 'Don't worry.'

I can't help worrying though. So far, my birth month hasn't gone like I had planned,

and I don't want anything to mess up my
class party. 'Can we check the bag one
more time?'

Mum opens the shopping bag with all
the party supplies in it. Candles. Matches.
Happy Birthday plates and napkins. Mum's
camera, so she can take pictures for my
birth month scrapbook.

'Everything we need to make sure today
is the best-school-party-ever is in the bag,'
Mum says.

On the way to school, I tell Joey how excited I am. 'I don't know how I'm going to be able to wait all day,' I say as we walk into Room 310.

Joey looks at his watch. 'You actually only have to wait six hours.'

Maybe six hours isn't all day, but to me, it feels like it might as well be six years. I can't wait until this afternoon!

Before Mrs Daily makes everyone sit down, I tell my friends that my parents are bringing birthday fairy cakes at the end of the day.

'Oooh, I love fairy cakes,' squeals Danielle.

'Me too,' says Arielle.

'What kind are they?' asks Pamela.

'The yummy kind,' I tell Pamela. I want everyone to be surprised when they see my fairy cakes.

'Class, please take your seats,' says Mrs Daily. 'We have a lot to do today, and we have a birthday party at the end of the day.' Mrs Daily smiles at me, then she writes *Happy Birthday, Mallory* on the chalkboard.

'Mallory's real birthday is on Monday, but since there's no school on Monday, we're going to celebrate today.'

Mrs Daily tells us to open our maths books on page 112.

During maths, I try to focus on working, but I keep looking at the clock.

Every time I do, the hands remind me of candles, and I think about my class party at the end of the day.

Some school days go by slowly, but today is the slowest ever. I can hardly wait for 2.30 to get here.

When it finally does, I stop watching the clock and start watching the door. 'My parents should be here any minute,' I tell Pamela.

'Soon it will be lights, camera, fairy cakes!' she says.

I watch the door swing open and Mum walks in. She walks over to my desk and hugs me. 'You have everything,' I say looking into the shopping bag in her arms.

'Almost everything,' she says smiling. 'Dad should be here any minute with the fairy cakes.'

The door swings open again and Dad walks in, but his hands are empty. 'Where are the fairy cakes?' I ask when he comes over to my desk.

Dad pats me on the head. 'Sweetheart, Mum has the fairy cakes.'

I look at Dad. 'She said *you* were bringing them.'

Dad looks at Mum. 'Sherry, you have the fairy cakes, right?'

Mum shakes her head. 'Harry, you were supposed to stop at the cake shop on the way here and pick them up.'

'I thought you were bringing everything,' says Dad. Mum and Dad start whispering to each other.

If they are playing a birthday joke on me, it's not funny. 'Who brought the fairy cakes?' I ask softly. I know somebody has to have the fairy cakes, because you can't have a party without them.

Dad puts his hands on my shoulders. He has a funny look on his face. 'Sweet Potato, I'm afraid Mum and I had a little mix-up.'

'Is there a problem?' Mrs Daily asks.

Mum explains to Mrs Daily that Dad was supposed to pick up the fairy cakes, but he thought she was bringing them.

'You mean no one brought the fairy cakes?!?' I say.

Mum and Dad don't say anything, but I know the answer. There are no lights.

There are no cameras. THERE ARE NO
FAIRY CAKES!

'Can't Dad go and get them?' I ask.

Mrs Daily looks at me. 'Mallory, school
ends soon. There's not enough time for
your dad to go and get the fairy cakes and
bring them back in time to have a party.'

'I've got some mints in my purse,' says
Mum. 'Why don't I pass out mints to

everyone, and we can still sing *Happy Birthday?*'

I sit down at my desk. 'You can't put a candle in a mint,' I say to Mum.

'I've got some crisps,' says Joey.

'You can't stick a candle in a crisp, either,' I tell him.

'How about half a tuna sandwich from my lunch?' says Pamela. 'We could stick a candle in that.'

I look down at the floor. I don't want everyone to sing *Happy Birthday* to me over mints or crisps or tuna fish. I want my pink and white fairy cakes.

Mrs Daily puts her arm around me. 'We don't need fairy cakes to celebrate your birthday. Class, let's all sing *Happy Birthday* to Mallory.'

I try to smile while my class sings, but inside, I don't feel very smiley.

Dad puts his arm around me. 'Mallory, Mum and I made a mistake, and we are really sorry.' He hugs me. 'I feel like a real party pooper,' says Dad.

'Me too,' says Mum.

Me three. I feel like my party pooped before it ever popped.

Joey comes over to me. 'Hey, at least Mary Ann will be here tonight.'

I try to smile. I know Mum and Dad didn't mean to forget the fairy cakes, and I know Joey is trying to make me feel better, but so far, my birth month celebration has been a big, fat flop.

At least Joey's right about one thing: Mary Ann is coming tonight, and when she gets here, I just know everything will get better.

It can't get any worse.

MALLORY GETS
A MAKEOVER

I line up bottles and jars, brushes and combs on my bathroom sink. Then I look at my watch. 'Cheeseburger,' I say, 'we've got a lot to do and not much time to do it.'

Mary Ann and her mum will be here in less than an hour. The Winstons are coming over for a pre-birthday dinner.

Tonight is the official start of my birth

weekend, and it's not just a regular birth weekend. There's no school on Monday, so it's a three-day-long birth weekend.

Even though my class party was a flop, I know tonight will be great. And I want to look great. I want to look like I'm turning nine on Monday because on Monday . . . I AM TURNING NINE!!!

I look at Cheeseburger. 'Why don't we start with make-up.' Mum usually won't let me wear make-up, but she said I could put on a little since tonight is a special occasion.

I brush sparkly peach blusher on my cheeks. I coat my lips with shiny pink lip gloss. I even put a dab of shimmery blue shadow on my eyelids. Then I paint my nails with pale yellow polish and blow on them, so they'll dry quickly.

'How do I look?' I ask Cheeseburger.

She purrs. I take that as a good sign. 'Now it's time for hair,' I say.

I open up my drawer with all my hair thingies in it. I take out a pair of hairgrips. I pull back a little hair on each side of my face and clip in the hairgrips.

I look in the mirror. This doesn't look like a nine-year-old hairstyle. I rip out the hairgrips and pull my hair into a ponytail on top of my head.

When I look in the mirror, I don't like what I see. 'This doesn't even look like an eight-year-old hairstyle,' I mumble to Cheeseburger.

I take out the ponytail, fluff up my fringe, and put a little gel on the ends. I even try twisting the ends into little curls. I still don't like what I see.

'Cheeseburger, what I need is a nine-year-old makeover. Any ideas?' But when I look at Cheeseburger, she's asleep on top of the toilet.

I try rubbing my forehead with my little fingers. That's what I always do when I'm trying to think of a good idea. But today, it's not so easy to rub my forehead with my pinkies, because my forehead is covered up with fringe.

I try pushing my fringe to the side, but it falls back down onto my face.

And that's when I get an idea. NOT being able to rub my forehead gives me a great idea. What I need is less hair on my forehead. I stare into the mirror and try to imagine what I would look like if my fringe wasn't so long.

What I imagine is me, but not eight-year-old me. I see nine-year-old Mallory. I walk over to my desk and get my scissors. 'I'm just going to cut a little off the bottom,' I say to Cheeseburger when I'm back in the bathroom.

I start on the left side of my forehead and work my way to the right. When I'm finished, I look in the mirror. The left side looks a little longer than the right side.

I cut a little more off the left, just to even it up, but when I'm done, the left side looks a little shorter to me than the right side.

Cutting my fringe isn't as easy as I thought it would be.

I nudge Cheeseburger so she'll wake up.

She opens her eyes. 'Cheeseburger, I need a second opinion.' I point to the right side of my fringe. 'Does this side look a little shorter to you?'

Cheeseburger purrs. I take that as a *yes*.
I snip some hair off the bottom of the right
side of my fringe.

Now the right side looks MUCH shorter
than the left, and I don't need a second
opinion to know that.

I pull the left side of my fringe into a
chunk and start snipping.

When I'm finished, I look in the mirror.
What I would like to see is a fringe that is

even on the left side and the right side. But what I see is NO fringe on the left side.

'CHEESEBURGER!' I scream. 'LOOK AT MY HAIR!'

Cheeseburger jumps when I scream, and she looks at me. I can tell by the way she's looking that she thinks something is wrong.

I can't have half a fringe. I grab the scissors and snip off the right half of my fringe to try to make things even.

When I'm finished, I look in the mirror. Now I don't have any fringe at all! I don't look like *nine-year-old* Mallory. I look like a Ping-Pong ball. I reach up to feel the spot where my fringe used to be. It feels prickly.

'This is awful!' I tell Cheeseburger. I can't believe I cut my whole fringe off . . . right when Mary Ann is coming to town, right before my birthday.

I can feel my eyes filling up with tears.

'Oh, Cheeseburger!' I moan. 'What am I going to do?'

But Cheeseburger just stares at the pile of hair on the floor that used to be my fringe.

'Mary Ann is going to be here any minute. I don't want anyone to see me like this, not even my best friend,' I tell Cheeseburger. Tears roll down my cheeks.

There's only one thing I can do. I go into my bedroom and lock the door.

I'm staying in my room forever . . . or at least until my fringe grows back. I try to think how long it will take.

One time when I got a haircut, the hairdresser told me that hair grows a centimetre a month. I try to measure my forehead with my index finger. It's about six centimetres long, which means I'll be stuck in my room for at least four months.

If I'm stuck in here for that long, I could starve! I'm hungry already.

'Mallory!' Mum yells from the kitchen. 'Mary Ann is here.'

I pull aside my curtains and look outside. Mary Ann's mum's car is in the driveway. I see the Winstons walking over. I close my curtains. I don't want any of them to see me.

I hear everyone inside my house.

'Mallory!' Mum calls my name again.

I hear footsteps running down the hall.

'Mallory! Open up! I'm here! ' says a familiar voice on the other side of my door.

I reach up and rub my prickly spot. I can't let Mary Ann see me like this.

'Mallory? Are you in there?'

I don't answer. I hear Mary Ann going back down the hall.

Then I hear more footsteps and voices

coming towards my room. 'Mallory, open up.'

'I can't come out,' I tell Dad.

'Why not?' Dad sounds concerned.

'I can't tell you why, but trust me, I can't.'

'She has to come out,' Mary Ann says to Dad.

'C'mon,' says Dad. 'Everyone's here. Mary Ann, Joey, Winnie. It's time for your pre-birthday dinner.'

'I'm not coming out,' I tell Dad. 'Not now. Not for a long time.'

'Mallory,' says Dad. 'I'm going to count to three, and I want you to open this door.'

Dad counts, but I don't open the door.

'Mallory Louise McDonald, open this door this instant!' says Dad.

I don't.

'I think your dad went to get your mum,' says Mary Ann.

She's right. Mum is at my door in less time than it takes to cut off your fringe. 'Mallory, what's wrong? You need to come out of your room. We want to start dinner, and we can't start without you.'

I don't answer Mum. I just curl up on my bed next to Cheeseburger.

'Mallory, I'm not going to ask again. You need to come out of your room now, and if you don't, we're starting without you.'

I think about the cheeseburgers Dad is cooking on the grill. I think about the fairy cakes and ice cream Mum is serving for dessert. I think about how much fun it would be to celebrate my birthday with my family and friends.

Then I think about my hair. I can hear what Max would say if he saw me without my fringe. *If you look up the word ugly in the dictionary, you'd see Mallory's picture next to it.*

'Start without me,' I tell Mum.

I pull Cheeseburger close to me. 'It's just you and me,' I tell her, 'for the next four months.'

A PYJAMA PARTY

Mary Ann bangs on my door. 'C'mon,' she says. 'Open up. I've been here for two hours and I haven't even seen you yet.'

I want to see my best friend, but I don't want her to see me. 'I'm not opening my door,' I tell Mary Ann.

'Why not?' she asks.

'I can't tell you why not.'

'But I'm your best friend,' says Mary Ann. 'You can tell me anything. We came here to celebrate your birthday and I can't celebrate if I can't see you!'

'Mallory, open up right now,' says Dad. I watch my doorknob rattle.

I know I can't stay locked in my room forever. Mary Ann is my best friend, and she did come to celebrate my birthday. I take my snow hat out of the closet and pull it down over my forehead. I open my door.

When I do, Mum, Dad, Max, Mary Ann, and her mum are all standing there.

They walk into my room. 'What's going on?' asks Mum. She looks suspicious.

Mary Ann gives me a hug. 'Your pre-birthday dinner wasn't much fun without you.' Then she gets a funny look on her face. 'Why are you wearing your hat inside?'

Before I can stop her, Mary Ann reaches
up and pulls my hat off my head.

'MALLORY?' Mum says my name like
she's not sure she recognizes me.

Mary Ann puts her hands on her cheeks.
'Mallory, where is your fringe?'

I cover my forehead with one hand and

point towards my bathroom with the other. 'On the floor in there,' I say.

Max laughs. 'I never thought I'd say this, but they looked better on than off.'

'Max, that's enough.' Mum gives Max a sharp look. Then she walks over to me and inspects what's left of my hair. 'Sweetie, why did you cut your fringe?' Mum asks.

I explain that my makeover didn't turn out like I thought it would. When I've finished talking, Mum puts her arm around me. 'It's really not a big deal. Your hair will grow back before you know it.'

Dad smiles at me. 'Just think of all the money we'll save on shampoo.'

I know Dad is trying to make me laugh, but I'm not in the mood for jokes.

'I think you look cute and grown up.' Mary Ann's mum puts one arm around me and the other around Mary Ann. 'Now why don't we get out of here and let you two catch up with each other.'

I might have lost my fringe, but at least I still have my best friend. 'That sounds great,' I say.

After everyone leaves, I look at Mary Ann. 'What am I going to do?'

'We're going to find a new hairstyle for you,' says Mary Ann.

'Do you really think we can?'

Mary Ann nods. 'Of course we can!'

I hug her. 'You're the best, best, best friend in the whole wide world.'

Mary Ann grins. 'Let's put on our pyjamas first and we'll have a *Find-a-new-hairstyle-for-Mallory* pyjama party.'

Now it's my turn to grin. Mary Ann knows I love pyjama parties!

Mary Ann pulls her penguin pyjamas out of her suitcase. I put on my matching ones,

then scoop up Cheeseburger and follow
Mary Ann into the bathroom.

She opens my hair-thingies drawer and
pulls out handfuls of ribbons, headbands
and clips. 'We're going to have to
experiment until we find the right hairstyle
for you.' Mary Ann picks up a purple ribbon
and ties it into a big bow
on the front of my head.

I look in the mirror,
but when I see myself, I
shut my eyes. 'I look like
an overgrown baby,' I
tell Mary Ann.

Mary Ann looks at my
reflection in the mirror,
then unties the bow. I open one eye and
watch while she pins in butterfly clips all
over the front of my head.

'What do you think?' asks Mary Ann.

I look in the mirror. 'I think I look like the butterfly exhibit at the zoo.'

'Hmmm,' says Mary Ann. 'I see what you mean.' She takes the clips out. 'Let's try this.' She pushes a thick striped headband over the front of my head.

I look in the mirror and smile. 'I like it!'

Cheeseburger purrs. 'I think Cheeseburger likes it too,' says Mary Ann. She smiles. 'You look cute with or without a fringe,' she says.

When I cut off my fringe, I thought tonight would be a total disaster, but it turned out OK. I throw my arms around Mary Ann. 'This has been our best pyjama party ever.'

Mary Ann nods, like she agrees.

'We'll have to go headband shopping,' I say to Mary Ann. I start thinking about all my different outfits. 'I'll need a red one and a purple one and a green one and a blue one. Maybe we'll go tomorrow,' I say.

Mary Ann grins. 'I can't believe I forgot to tell you what's happening tomorrow.'

I try to think what could be happening tomorrow. Tomorrow is Saturday. My skating party isn't until Monday. Maybe Mum planned something else on Saturday for my birth month celebration.

'Are you sure it's OK to tell me?' I ask Mary Ann. 'I wouldn't want to spoil any surprises.'

Mary Ann smiles even bigger than when she found the perfect hairstyle for me. 'I think you'll be surprised when you hear this. Tonight at dinner, my mum and Joey's dad sat next to each other.'

I shrug my shoulders. 'What's the big

deal about them sitting next to each other?'

'I think they liked sitting next to each other, because tomorrow night, they're going out on a date. Isn't that great?' squeals Mary Ann.

I rub my ear. 'I guess so,' I say.

'Think about it,' says Mary Ann. 'Joey's mum died, so Joey's dad is all alone, and since my parents are divorced, my mum is all alone.' Mary Ann smiles. 'If you ask me, they make the perfect pair.'

If you ask me, there is nothing perfect about it.

If Mary Ann's mum and Joey's dad go out on a date, they might fall in love.

If they fall in love, they might decide to get married.

If they get married, Mary Ann and Joey will become step-brother and sister.

If they become step-brother and sister, they will do all kinds of things, like live in the same house together and eat all their meals together and go on family holidays together, and they will do all these things . . . WITHOUT ME!

Mary Ann taps me on the head. 'Isn't it so, so, so great that my mum and Joey's dad are going out on a date?'

I nod my head yes, that I do think it is

great. But I don't think it's great at all. In fact, I think it is terrible, even worse than cutting off my fringe. Mary Ann and her mum came to see me on my birthday. They didn't come so Mary Ann's mum could go out on a date with Joey's dad.

Mary Ann and I get into bed, and she reaches up and turns off the light. 'Watch out for bedbugs!' says Mary Ann.

I say it back, because that's what we always say to each other at pyjama parties, but as I put my head on my pillow, I don't think about bedbugs. I think about our pyjama party, and all I can think is that the best-pyjama-party-ever just turned into the worst-pyjama-party-ever.

HIGHS AND WOES

'Who wants pizza and who wants . . . ' Crystal, our Saturday-night babysitter, looks around the kitchen, then finishes her sentence. 'Pizza?' She laughs at her joke. She knows all there is to pick from is pizza.

'I'll have the . . . ' Joey pretends to consider his choices. 'Pizza,' he says in a funny voice. Then he cracks up.

'Hmmm,' says Mary Ann, like she can't decide what she wants. 'I think I'll have . . . pizza too.' She laughs along with Joey.

Even Winnie and Max smile like they think the whole pizza thing is funny.

'Everyone certainly is in a good mood tonight,' says Crystal.

Make that *almost* everyone.

I must be the only kid on Wish Pond Road who is not in a good mood. I pull my headband down over my forehead.

'Guess who's going out on a date tonight?' Joey says to Crystal.

Crystal puts a slice of pizza on a paper plate. 'Give me a hint.'

'He lives in my house. He's bald. And he's not my grandfather,' says Joey.

Crystal laughs. 'Gee, this is a tough one. I would say your dad, but he never goes out on dates.'

'He is tonight,' says Mary Ann. 'He's going out with my mum!'

Crystal pretends like she's looking into a crystal ball. 'I see an expensive restaurant. I see flowers. I see candles. I see true love!'

Crystal thinks she is a fortune-teller.

Sometimes, I think she knows what she's

talking about, but not this time. She can't know that Joey's dad and Mary Ann's mum are going to fall in love. She just met Mary Ann and her mum tonight for the first time.

I take a slice of pizza out of the box, go into the living room, and sit down on the couch with Cheeseburger.

Maybe Mary Ann, Joey, Winnie, Max and even Crystal are happy about Mary Ann's mum and Joey's dad going out on a date, but I'm not.

My mum and Mary Ann's mum spent the whole day talking about it.

What should Mary Ann's mum wear? How should she do her hair? What colour should she paint her nails?

Dad was on the phone all afternoon trying to make a reservation at a restaurant.

Did they want French? Or maybe

Italian? Should they go at seven or at eight?

Mary Ann and Joey and Winnie talked all day about their parents going out.

What if they like each other? What if they really, really, really like each other?

All anybody talked about today was 'The Date'. But if you ask me, they were talking about the wrong date. The date they should have been talking about is my birth date. It seems like everyone around here has forgotten that I'm turning nine in two days.

Especially Mary Ann! She came here to celebrate my birthday, and I think she has forgotten that I'm even having one.

I take a bite of pizza. I hear everyone in the kitchen laughing. I rub Cheeseburger's back. 'I guess it's just you and me,' I say to my cat.

'Hey,' says Crystal. She sits down beside me. 'Why the gloomy face?'

I shrug my shoulders and take another bite of pizza.

Crystal looks at me, then she pretends to look into her crystal ball again.

But I don't give her a chance to predict my future. 'It's like this,' I explain to Crystal. 'My birthday is on Monday. This is my birthday weekend and not one single thing is going the way it's supposed to.'

Crystal starts to say something, but I don't let her.

'And to make matters worse, everyone is having a good time. Everyone except for one person and that one person is ME!'

'Mallory,' Crystal says, but I stop her. I pull my headband down on my forehead and point to the spot where my fringe used to be.

Crystal looks me in the eye. 'Mallory,

your fringe will grow back, and I don't need a crystal ball to tell me what's wrong with you. What you have is a bad case of highs and woes.'

I'm not sure I want to know, but I ask anyway. 'What are highs and woes?'

'Think of it like this,' Crystal explains. 'Sometimes when you feel good, you feel like you're high up in the air. It seems like your feet are barely touching the ground, and your head is way up in the clouds. And sometimes, when you feel bad, you feel low, like your whole body is crawling around in the dirt.'

Sometimes I think Crystal is the weirdest babysitter in Fern Falls. 'Well, wouldn't that be called *highs and lows, not highs and woes?*' I ask Crystal.

Crystal shakes her head, like she's an old, wise woman who's about to explain something to me. 'You have to understand the difference between *lows* and *woes*.'

I raise an eyebrow. Crystal is going to tell me the difference between *lows* and *woes*, whether I want to know or not.

'*Lows* are when you feel badly about something, but *woes* are different. *Woes* are when you feel badly about something and everybody else feels good about it, which makes you feel even worse.' Crystal gets a serious look on her face. 'Do you understand what I'm saying?'

I rub my forehead. 'I suppose so,' I mumble without looking up. Somehow listening to Crystal tell me I have *woes* makes me feel even worse.

Crystal puts her arm around me. 'Cheer up, Mal,' she says.

'I'll try,' I tell Crystal.

But I feel woe . . . as woe as you can go.

BIRTHDAY WISHES

I run my fingers through the pebbles on the edge of the wish pond. I see white and grey pebbles. What I don't see are shiny, little black pebbles, otherwise known as wish pebbles.

When I moved to Wish Pond Road, Joey told me that when you find a wish pebble and throw it into the wish pond, your wish is supposed to come true.

It sounds simple, but wish pebbles are hard to find, especially when you need one, and right now, I need one.

I pick up the closest thing I can find that looks like a wish pebble. I close my eyes and start to make a wish, but when I do, my wish turns into a wish list.

I wish my birth month had gone like I had planned it to.

I wish I hadn't cut off my fringe.

I wish Mary Ann's mum and Joey's dad hadn't gone out on a date.

I wish they won't go out on another one.

I start to throw my stone in the wish pond, then I think about my skating party tomorrow. Even though my wish list is long, I add another one to it.

I wish Mum had planned a surprise party for me. I can't help thinking about how much fun it would be to walk into a party and be super surprised.

I squeeze the stone in the palm of my hand. I'm about to throw it in the wish pond when I hear someone sit down beside me. I open one eye. It's Dad. 'How did you know I was here?' I ask him.

Dad sits down beside me. 'I heard the front door open. Mum, Max, Mary Ann, her mum, Champ and Cheeseburger were all asleep in their beds. The only person I couldn't find was you. I thought you might be out here.'

I cross my arms.

'What are you doing out here by yourself so early in the morning?'

'Making wishes,' I tell Dad.

Dad picks up a stone and throws it into the pond. 'Feel like talking about what you're wishing for?'

I look down at the pebble in my hand. 'If I tell, my wishes might not come true.'

'Sometimes talking about things is better than wishing for them,' says Dad.

I close my fingers around the pebble in my hand. 'I don't know where to start.'

'How about the beginning?' says Dad.

I think about my wish list. My long, long, long wish list. Then I take a deep breath and start. 'I worked so hard to plan the perfect birth month celebration,' I tell Dad. 'And nothing happened like it was supposed to.'

'Mallory, I know you expected things to happen a certain way during your birth

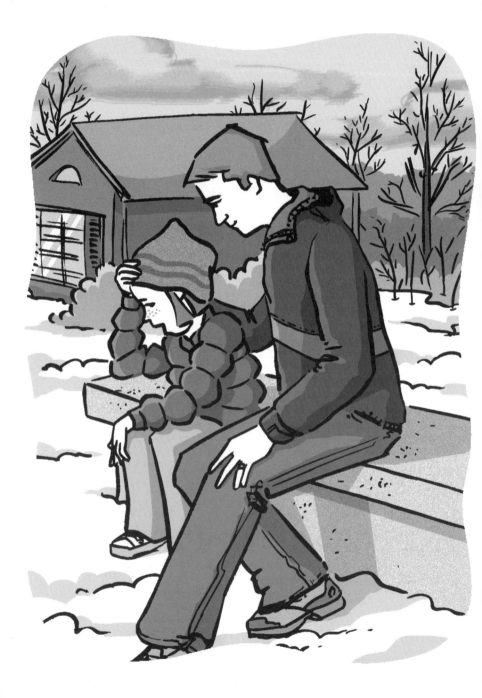

month, and they didn't. I know that's disappointing.'

'That's not all.' I reach up and feel my forehead. 'I was just trying to look like a nine-year-old and look what happened to my hair.'

Dad puts his arm around me. 'Sweet Potato, it'll grow back.'

Then I tell Dad how scared I am about Mary Ann's mum and Joey's dad liking each other. 'I wish they hadn't gone out on a date.'

'But they did,' says Dad. 'And you can't change that.'

'Did they have a good time?' I cross my toes and hope Dad says *no*.

But he nods his head *yes*. 'They had a very nice time together,' says Dad.

This is not what I wanted to hear.

'Do you think they'll go out again?' I ask.

Dad looks down at me. 'Yes, I do.'

I kick my foot against a pile of rocks on the side of the wish pond. 'What if they fall in love and get married, and Mary Ann and Joey become brother and sister, and they're together all the time without me?'

'Sweet Potato, there are some things you can control and some things you can't. When you can't control something, you just have to accept it.'

Dad tilts my face up so I'm looking at him. 'Do you understand what I'm trying to tell you?'

I shake my head, *no*. I'm not sure I do.

'Mallory, things didn't happen the way you expected them to. You might wish that things could have been different, but you can't change what happened.'

I think about what Dad said. I can't change what happened during my birth month. I can't make my fringe reappear. I can't do anything about the fact that Mary Ann's mum and Joey's dad went out on a date, and that they might go out on another one.

But there is something I *can* change.

'Thanks Dad, you gave me a great idea!'

Dad smiles at me. 'Glad I could help.'

I stand up and start to go home. Then I stop.

I squeeze the rock in my hand, then throw it into the wish pond. *I wish my birthday party will be the best surprise party in the whole world.*

And I'm planning to make sure that it is.

MALLORY ON HER OWN

'You want to plan your own surprise party?'

'No,' I explain to Mary Ann. 'I want *you* to plan it.' I sit down on the bed next to her, 'and I'll be your assistant.'

Mary Ann looks confused. 'But if you're my assistant, everybody will know that you know about the surprise.'

'That's the thing,' I whisper to Mary Ann. 'No one will know I'm your assistant . . . no one but you.'

Mary Ann winks at me. 'I get it. You're going to be my *secret* assistant.'

'Exactly!' I say. Then I stop to think for a minute. 'There's just one more problem. How are you going to tell my mum that you're planning a surprise party when she's already planned a skating party?'

'Simple,' says Mary Ann. 'I'll tell her that you really want a surprise party and as your lifelong best friend, I want to make one for you.'

Mary Ann makes it sound simple, but I'm not sure it will be. 'Don't you think my mum will be upset when she finds out I don't want to have the party she planned?'

Mary Ann shrugs. 'I'm sure she'll understand when I explain it to her.'

I'm not so sure Mum will understand. She didn't understand when I told her I wanted to celebrate my birth month. She didn't understand when I said I wanted to get my ears pierced. I'm not sure she'll understand this either.

Mary Ann leans over and taps me on the head with a pencil. 'Earth to Mallory. We've got a lot to do to plan a surprise party before tomorrow.'

She closes the door to my room and sits down at my desk. 'Let's make a list of everything we need.'

I sit down on my bed with Cheeseburger. Mary Ann starts writing.

'Invitations,' says Mary Ann. 'We need to tell everybody that your party has changed from a skating party to a surprise party.'

'We can make our own.' I show Mary Ann a picture in a magazine of party invitations shaped like paper fans.

Mary Ann claps her hands together when she sees it. 'They'll be so cute!'

I nod. They will be cute, but there's a problem. 'How will we get them to people in time for the party?'

Mary Ann rubs her chin. 'Joey can deliver them for us.'

'Now, let's talk about food,' says Mary Ann.

'I can make peanut butter and marshmallow sandwiches and lemonade,' I say.

'You better let me make them,' says Mary Ann. 'You don't want anyone to see you making your own party food.'

Mary Ann is right. I don't want to spoil my own surprise. 'But we still need a cake,' I remind her. 'Do you know how to bake a cake?'

Mary Ann scratches her head. 'Your mum will bring the cake. When I tell her about the party, I'll remind her to bring the cake.' Mary Ann looks down at the piece of paper in her lap. 'What about party gifts?'

I reach over and open the drawer to my bedside table.

I take out a bookmark with a big *M* on it. 'We can make bookmarks with everyone's initials on them and then decorate them with glitter and bows.'

'Great idea!' says Mary Ann. 'There's just one thing left to do.'

'What's that?' I ask.

Mary Ann lowers her voice. 'We have to work out how we're going to surprise you.'

I think for a minute. Working out how to surprise myself is harder than making invitations and party gifts.

I snap my fingers. 'I've got it. I'll pretend like I'm getting ready for my skating party. When it's time to go, I'll walk into the living room in my skating clothes and you'll have everybody waiting there to surprise me.'

'Perfect!' says Mary Ann. She looks at her watch. 'We better get busy or we won't get everything done by tomorrow. I'll go talk to your mum and Joey. You start folding fans.'

Mary Ann leaves my room. I reach into my drawer, take out thick sheets of construction paper and start folding.

Part of me can't wait to be surprised. But part of me feels like planning my own surprise party might not be such a good idea. I hope Mum isn't upset when Mary Ann talks to her.

I keep folding fans. When Mary Ann comes back into my room, my bed is covered with colourful fans. 'Wow!' says Mary Ann. 'These look great.'

'Now all we have to do is write the party information on them, decorate them, and tie ribbons through the bottoms of them,' I tell her.

'Joey is ready to deliver them,' says Mary

Ann. 'And your mum is bringing the cake.'

I look up. 'Did my mum seem upset when you told her about the party?'

Mary Ann ties a ribbon through the bottom of a fan. 'She didn't say she was.'

I sprinkle glitter across a yellow fan. Just because Mum didn't say she was upset doesn't mean she's not. I really hope she understands that I want to have a surprise party, and I hope she's OK with that.

When we've finished making the invitations, Mary Ann takes them next door to Joey.

When she comes back, Mary Ann and I start on the bookmarks. We work all morning until Mum knocks on my door. 'Time for lunch, girls.'

'Remember,' I whisper to Mary Ann, 'not a word about this to my mum. I don't want her to know I'm in on this.'

Mary Ann holds up two fingers like she's making a promise. 'It's our secret.'

After lunch, Mary Ann and I go back to making bookmarks. 'Do you think we'll ever finish?' I ask her.

'Maybe you should finish in here,' says Mary Ann. 'I'll go and make the lemonade and sandwiches.' Mary Ann winks at me. 'I'll tell your mum you're taking a nap.'

By the time Mary Ann and I get ready for bed, we are both tired from all the party planning. 'Thanks for everything,' I tell Mary Ann as we put on our matching yellow peace-sign pyjamas. 'I thought I would have to plan my party on my own. But I should have known I could count on you.'

Mary Ann smiles at me. 'I think this will be the best surprise ever.' She turns off the light.

to go to sleep, but something is ......ing me. I turn the light back on.

Mary Ann sits up. 'What's the matter?'

'We forgot something,' I tell her.

Mary Ann shakes her head. 'We have invitations, gifts and food.'

'Clothes!' I say to Mary Ann. 'I'm the party girl and I need just the right outfit to look like I'm going skating.'

'Hmmm.' Mary Ann looks at me. 'Why don't you wear something yellow.'

'Good idea,' I say to Mary Ann. I get my yellow jeans and matching jumper out of my wardrobe. 'Yellow is a perfect party colour.'

Mary Ann nods, like she agrees. 'Watch out for bedbugs!' she says.

'You too,' I say, but I'm so tired from all our party planning that I don't think my eyes can stay open long enough to look for bedbugs. I turn out the light and put my head down on the pillow.

'Cheeseburger,' I whisper, 'I can't wait to be surprised.'

SURPRISES!

'Mallory, wake up!'

For a minute, I think I'm being attacked by bedbugs, but when I open my eyes, it's just Mum. 'What's the matter?' I ask her.

'Do you know what day it is today?' she asks me.

I have to think for a minute. 'Monday?'

'It's Monday,' says Mum. 'But do you know why this Monday is different than all other Mondays?'

I roll over and look at the clock on my bedside table. It's so early!

'Mum, on all other Mondays, we have school, but today we don't. What's so important about this Monday that you needed to wake me up so early?'

'I think you'll be very excited when you hear what I have to say.' Mum sits down on the bed beside me. 'Today is your birthday, and I have a surprise for you!'

I think about the surprise party I'm having this afternoon. 'A surprise?' I ask.

'Why don't I show you,' she says. Mum ties a bandanna around my eyes, then helps me out of bed. I can feel her leading me down the hall.

'Where are we going?' I ask. I can't imagine where she would be taking me so early in the morning in my pyjamas.

Mum stops walking. 'Would you like to

see your surprise?'

I nod. Mum unties the bandanna. When she takes it off, I am surprised . . . VERY SURPRISED!

'HAPPY BIRTHDAY, MALLORY!' shout my friends and my family.

Mum puts a party hat on my head. I look around the living room and can't believe what I'm seeing! Dad, Max, Mary Ann, her mum, Joey, Winnie, Mr Winston, Crystal, Pamela and all my friends from school are there . . . and they're all in their pyjamas and dressing gowns and slippers! Even Champ and Cheeseburger have on little matching nightcaps.

'What's going on?' I ask.

Mum grins. 'It's a surprise pyjama party for you! We all know how much you love pyjama parties.'

'And surprise parties!' says Mary Ann.

'But what about my skating party?'

Mum gives me a big hug. 'There never was a skating party.'

I can't believe it! 'There never was a skating party?'

Mum shakes her head. 'Dad and I wanted to make sure you would be really surprised.' I am really surprised *and* really confused.

'What about the party Mary Ann and I planned? What happened to the invitations we made?' I look at Joey. 'The ones you delivered yesterday?'

Joey smiles. 'I delivered the them. . . to your mum.'

'And I hid them in the kitchen,' Mum says.

I can't believe it. 'You knew about this?' I say to Joey.

He grins. 'I can be a very good secret keeper.'

There's another good secret keeper too. I look at Mary Ann. 'You knew about this and spent the whole day yesterday helping me make invitations and bookmarks and sandwiches. You didn't say a word.'

'Joey and I didn't want to spoil the real surprise. We were your mum's assistants.' She winks at me. 'Her secret assistants.'

I throw my arms around Mary Ann and Joey. 'You're the best friends a girl could have.'

Then I look at all my friends. 'You all knew about this and nobody said a word?'

Max smiles. 'I guess we're all good secret keepers.'

Mary Ann giggles. 'Look around.'

A sign on the wall says, *Happy Birthday, Mallory!* Streamers and balloons hang from the ceiling. There's a big pile of presents in the corner.

The dining room table is covered with all my favourite breakfast foods: doughnuts and hot chocolate with mini-marshmallows, even the plate of peanut butter and marshmallow sandwiches that Mary Ann made.

I pick one up and take a bite. 'Mmmmm.'

'Don't eat too many sandwiches,' says Mum. 'You need to save room for cake.' Dad carries in a tray with the biggest ice cream cake on it that I've ever seen.

'It's the cake-of-the-year,' says Dad. He puts the cake down on the table and lights the candles. Everybody sings *Happy*

Birthday.

'Make a wish,' says Mum.

I look at Dad, and we smile at each other. Yesterday at the wish pond, I wished for the best surprise party in the whole world. I close my eyes and blow out my candles. I feel like my wish is coming true.

Mum cuts the cake and Mary Ann's mum

passes around plates.

I take a bite. 'Mmmm! Cookies and cream for breakfast is my new favourite.'

Dad laughs. 'Ice cream for breakfast on birthdays only!'

'Time for games,' says Mum when everybody finishes their cake.

We play *Pin the Slippers on the Sheep.* It's like *Pin the Tail on the Donkey,* but you have to pin the slippers onto the sheep's feet.

Mum blindfolds Mary Ann and spins her around in a circle. Mary Ann walks towards the wall and pins the slippers on the sheep's nose.

When it's Joey's turn, he doesn't do much better. He pins the slippers on the sheep's ear, and Pamela pins them on his stomach.

Finally, Max pins the slippers in the right place . . . on the sheep's feet. Mum gives him a pair of fuzzy yellow slippers as a prize.

Max looks at the slippers like touching them could give him a bad disease. 'The birthday girl can have these.' He hands me the slippers.

I slip them on my feet. 'They look perfect with my pj's!'

I give Max a hug. 'You're the best brother a girl could have.'

Max rolls his eyes. 'On your birthday, only!'

When we finish playing *Pin the Slippers on the Sheep,* Mum holds up a glass jar of jelly beans. 'Who wants to play *Guess the Number of Jelly Beans in the Jar?'*

I look at the jar of jelly beans in Mum's hands. Then I look at the pile of presents.

It's hard to focus on jelly beans when they're near a pile of presents.

Pamela looks at me. 'I think the only game Mallory wants to play is called *Open the Presents!*'

I laugh. Pamela knows me really well. Then I give her a hug. 'You're the best classmate in all of Fern Falls!'

Mum piles all the boxes on the living room floor and everybody sits in a circle around me.

'Open this one first,' says Danielle. 'It's from Arielle and me.'

I open a big pink box filled with make-up. 'It's a make-up kit,' says Danielle. 'It's what you need if you want a new look.'

I thank Danielle and Arielle, but I give Mary Ann a secret smile. I've had enough new looks to last me for a while.

I keep opening presents. Mary Ann gives

me a ninth birthday scrapbook. It has nine
hearts on the cover. 'One for each year,'
says Mary Ann.

'I love it!' I tell her.

Joey and Winnie give me a new pair of
roller blades. 'Now you have your own
skates,' says Joey. 'And they're purple,'
says Winnie.

'Wow! I can't believe you got me these!'
I take off my fuzzy yellow slippers and try

on my new roller blades.

'Now we can go skating,' says Joey.

I grin. 'Sounds like fun.'

I keep opening presents.

Pamela gives me a glow-in-the-dark paper weight. Crystal gives me a days-of-the-week set of headbands.

Mum and Dad give me new pyjamas with birthday cakes all over them. 'You can celebrate your birthday every time you wear these,' says Dad.

Then Max hands me a box. It's big, but it's not heavy. When I shake it, it doesn't make a sound. 'I can't imagine what's in here,' I say to my brother.

'It's not really for you,' says Max. 'But I think you'll like it.'

Now, I'm really curious. I rip off the wrapping paper and open the box. Inside, there's a new cat bed for Cheeseburger . . .

and it matches my bed!

'I love it!' I say to Max. I try to hug him. He ducks, so I miss, but he smiles at me.

'I hope you have a great year!' says Max.

Mum passes out the party gifts she bought. 'Mini torches,' she says, 'so you can read in your pyjamas in bed.'

Then Mary Ann gives everyone the bookmarks we made.

After all the guests have gone, Mum picks up the tray with the leftover birthday cake on it. 'Did you like your party?' she asks me.

I scratch my head, like I have to think hard to answer the question she just asked me. 'Well, it wasn't exactly what I expected.'

Dad looks concerned. 'Sometimes,' he says, 'you don't get what you expected.'

I stop scratching and start smiling. 'And

sometimes, what you get is even better than what you expected.'

Mum puts the cake down. She and Dad both smile.

I hug them both. 'Mum, Dad, thanks so much for everything. I loved my party.'

'Surprises are fun,' says Dad.

I smile at my parents. 'Especially when you're really surprised.'

'Speaking of surprises,' says Dad. 'There's another one, and I think I hear it outside.'

I run to the front window. Grandma's car is pulling into our drive. 'Grandma!' I scream.

Everyone follows me outside.

When Grandma gets out of her car, I fling myself around her. 'I can't believe it! *You're* what you sent for my birthday!'

Grandma hugs me so hard she crushes

my party hat. 'I didn't wear pyjamas, but I did bring your present . . . in person!' She hands me a box wrapped in purple tissue paper.

I shake the box, but it doesn't make a sound. I rip off the paper and open the lid. Inside, there's a pillow that has the number nine inside a big heart.

I hug my pillow. 'It's perfect,' I tell

Grandma. 'I've only been nine for a few minutes, but I love it already! It's definitely full of surprises.' I take a deep breath and try to straighten my squashed party hat. 'I never thought I'd say this, but I think I've had enough surprises for one day.'

Everyone laughs. Then Mary Ann's mum comes over to me. 'Actually,' she says, 'I have one more.' She hands me a small box.

I think about my new scrapbook. 'But Mary Ann already gave me a present.'

'This one's from me,' says Mary Ann's mum. 'And I think you'll really like it.'

I clutch the small box in my hands. When I shake it, something rattles. I don't know what's inside, but I can't wait to find out.

THE REST OF
THE HOLE STORY

When I get to school, I hand Mrs Daily
a sheet of paper. 'You didn't ask me to
write this, but I thought you might like
reading it.'

'I'm always proud of my students when
they do extra work,' says Mrs Daily. Then
she smiles at me. 'And I can't wait to read
the rest of the story!'

The Rest of the Hole Story
by Mallory McDonald
NTR (No Tissues Required)

I know you must remember our story, which ended when the heroine was wiping away her tears because her mother refused to grant her one, actually two, small requests she made on her ninth birthday.

I'm sure you can't forget that whole you-have-to-wait-until-you're-twelve-to-get-your-ears-pierced speech.

Well, after the girl was forced to listen to that speech, she went to her room. Actually, she was sent there.

She made a wish for a miracle to happen and to her surprise and amazement, it did! Her fairy godmother (actually her lifelong best friend's mother) gave her a pair of earrings for her birthday.

Of course, the little girl gave them right back and said she didn't need them because her mother wouldn't let her get her ears pierced.

The girl's fairy godmother just smiled and told her that she explained to the girl's mother that waiting until you're twelve to get your ears pierced, especially when you've just cut off your fringe, didn't seem necessary.

And the girl's mother agreed!!! (I hope you didn't faint when you read this!)

So the fairy godmother drove the girl and the girl's best friend into town. (Unfortunately, they had to go in a car, not in a golden coach, but what happened next was so exciting, the girl didn't care.)

When she got into town, she got her ears pierced!

And everybody lived happily ever after. Especially the girl.

The End

P.S. In most fairy tales, the heroine falls in love with a handsome prince, but in this one, the fairy godmother falls for the man next door. At first, the heroine was pretty upset about this. She was worried about what it meant for her future. But her fairy godmother told the heroine to stop worrying about the future and start picking earrings, and that's exactly what the heroine did. She picked out heart-shaped earrings and so did her best friend. They promised to always wear matching earrings.

MALLORY'S PARTY PLANNING KIT

Birthdays are a big deal! Here are some things you can do to make your birthday party extra special!

INVITATIONS

You can make your own invitations shaped like fans. Just follow these four simple steps:

Step 1: Fold a piece of paper into the shape of a fan.

Step 2: On the folds of the paper, write the time, date and place of your party.

Step 3: Decorate your invitations with paint, markers and stickers.

Step 4: Deliver your invitations to your friends!

PARTY GIFTS

Handmade bookmarks are super cool. Just cut out paper in the shape of a bookmark. Then draw each guest's initial on the bookmark. Decorate the bookmarks with ribbons and glitter. Every time your friends open their books, they will remember your great party.

THANK-YOU NOTES

Don't forget the thank-you notes! I think the *fill-in-the-blank* ones are the best. You can decorate them so they match your invitations. Here's what mine looked like:

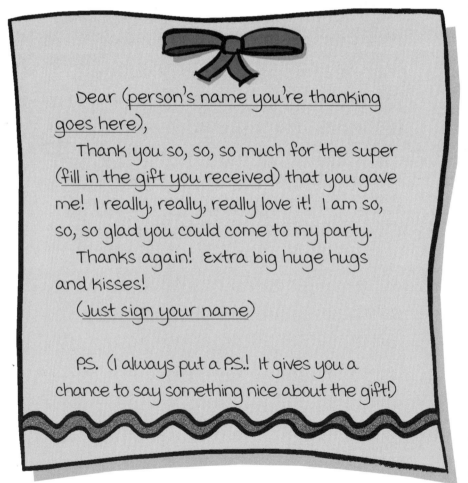

Dear (person's name you're thanking goes here),

Thank you so, so, so much for the super (fill in the gift you received) that you gave me! I really, really, really love it! I am so, so, so glad you could come to my party.

Thanks again! Extra big huge hugs and kisses!

(Just sign your name)

P.S. (I always put a P.S.! It gives you a chance to say something nice about the gift!)

And if you're thinking that writing thank-you notes isn't as much fun as other activities (like getting presents), you and I think a lot alike! But you have to do it. And you have to do it pretty soon after your party, or your mother (if she's anything like mine) will start saying: '*(Fill in your name here!), have you written those notes yet?*'

Trust me, you don't want your mum to start saying that!

Well, I hope you like some of these ideas, and I hope when your birthday rolls around it is super special! I know mine was.

I'm already thinking about my next birthday. I know it's a year away, but I'm turning ten, which is a VERY big deal!

I just love birthdays! Don't you?

First published in the United Kingdom in 2009 by
Lerner Books,
Dalton House,
60 Windsor Avenue,
London SW19 2RR

Website address: www.lernerbooks.co.uk

This edition was updated and edited for UK publication by Discovery Books Ltd.,
First Floor, 2 College Street, Ludlow, Shropshire SY8 1AN

British Library Cataloguing in Publication Data

Friedman, Laurie B., 1964–
Happy birthday, Mallory. – (Mallory)
1. Birthdays – Juvenile fiction 2. Children's stories
1. Title
813.6[J]

ISBN-13: 978 0 7613 4289 2

First published in the United States of America in 2005

Printed in Singapore